MEET ME on MERCER STREET

WRITTEN AND
ILLUSTRATED BY
BOOKI VIVAT

WITH COLOR BY
JOAN WIROLINGGO

SCHOLASTIC PRESS
NEW YORK

All rights reserved. Published by Scholastic Press, an imprint of Scholastic Inc.,
Publishers since 1920. SCHOLASTIC, SCHOLASTIC PRESS, and associated logos are trademarks
and/or registered trademarks of Scholastic Inc.

The publisher does not have any control over and does not assume any responsibility
for author or third-party websites or their content.

No part of this publication may be reproduced, stored in a retrieval system, or
transmitted in any form or by any means, electronic, mechanical, photocopying,
recording, or otherwise, without written permission of the publisher. For
information regarding permission, write to Scholastic Inc., Attention: Permissions
Department, 557 Broadway, New York, NY 10012.

This book is a work of fiction. Names, characters, places, and incidents are
either the product of the author's imagination or are used fictitiously, and any
resemblance to actual persons, living or dead, business establishments, events, or
locales is entirely coincidental.

Library of Congress Cataloging-in-Publication Data available

ISBN 978-1-338-78868-6 (paperback)
ISBN 978-1-338-78870-9 (hardcover)

10 9 8 7 6 5 4 3 2 1   24 25 26 27 28

Printed in China   62

First printing 2024
Book design by Cassy Price
Munich 1912 font by Roman Muradov

For all the neighbors and
neighborhoods I've called home

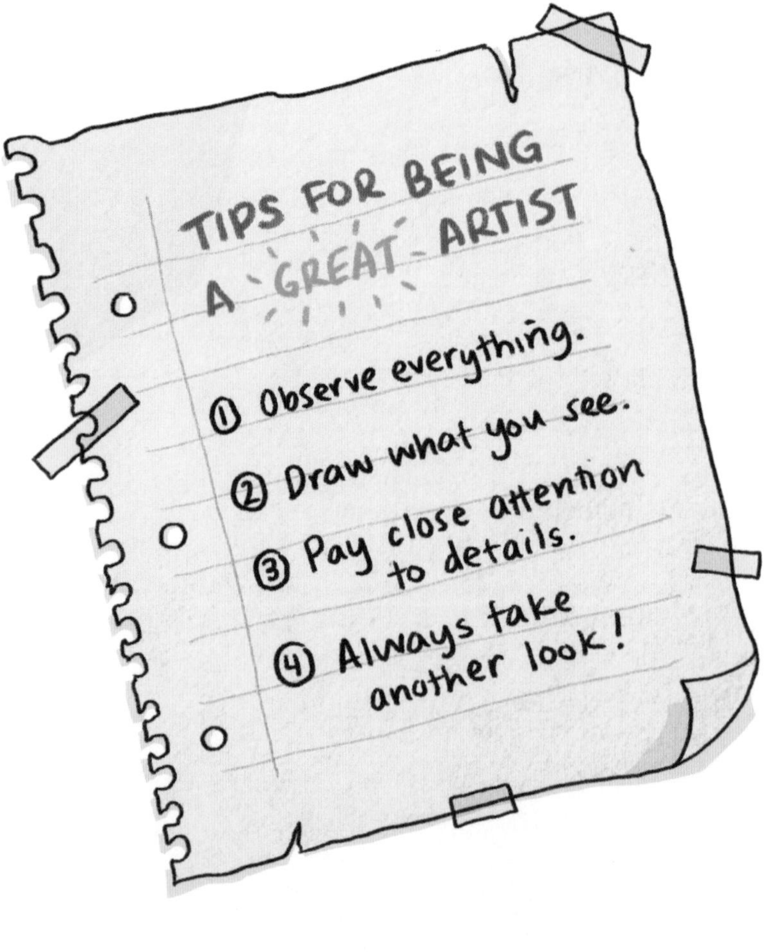
TIPS FOR BEING
A GREAT ARTIST
① Observe everything.
② Draw what you see.
③ Pay close attention to details.
④ Always take another look!

CHAPTER 1

Some people say you should mind your own business, but I want to be a great artist, and the key is seeing things that other people may not notice.

The best artists have a way of the looking at the world and using their art to show you something worth seeing.

A few years ago, my favorite teacher, Ms. Jenkins, caught me doodling in class.

You have a good eye...

Now try this.

Instead of getting mad, she handed me a sketchbook and told me I should channel my observations into art.

That's when I started drawing everything I saw.

Now I have so many notebooks that I don't even know where to keep them all.

My parents don't understand why I need to draw *everything*, but Ms. Jenkins said that true artists find a way to capture life around them.

I can't help that MY life just isn't that interesting.

brings the business protection + blessings

the unclaimed items rack

tangled up hangers everywhere

fills the whole place with a clean laundry smell

Uncle Ott's "5 minute break"

the problem washer that's always leaking

how Smiley's keeps track of things— very old school

Our family owns Smiley's Cleaners, a laundry and dry cleaning business right on Mercer Street in the center of town.

Besides school and home, this is where I spend most of my time. I'd rather join an after-school club or play a sport or hang out at the mall like most of my classmates, but instead, I'm stuck *here*. Luckily, I'm not the only kid in the neighborhood.

This is my best friend,

Her dad owns Khanna's Grocery & Deli, which is right down the street from Smiley's.

MR. KHANNA
(Nisha's Dad)

Since our families have businesses on Mercer Street, they're always there—and so are we. Every weekday after school, most weekends, even holiday breaks!

I usually spend my summers at home with Nisha, wandering around Mercer Street and waiting for something interesting to happen. Since so many kids go out of town once school is over, it sometimes feels like we are the only ones left. But together, we always make the best of it.

This year was different, though.

I couldn't believe it when Mom and Dad told me I'd be going away this summer.

Finally, a real vacation!

Of course, I should've known that their idea of a vacation would be to send me to my cousins' house.

Some kids travel to exciting destinations or go away to camp or spend their holidays lounging on the beach.

SOS SEND HELP ASAP!

I had to survive the hottest part of the year stuck in a room with no air-conditioning and a pair of hormonal teenagers. All without my best friend!

The last time I saw Nisha was at the start of summer break.

We should have been celebrating...

SCHOOL'S OUT!

But all I could think about was being exiled to my cousins' house for two whole months!

This is SO UNFAIR!

A blow-up air mattress that definitely has a hole in it!

Terrible Wi-Fi and no AC!

Hands-down the smelliest cat in existence!

WORST SUMMER VACATION *EVER!!!*

Plus, I won't have anyone fun to hang out with.

This stinks.

It really, really stinks.

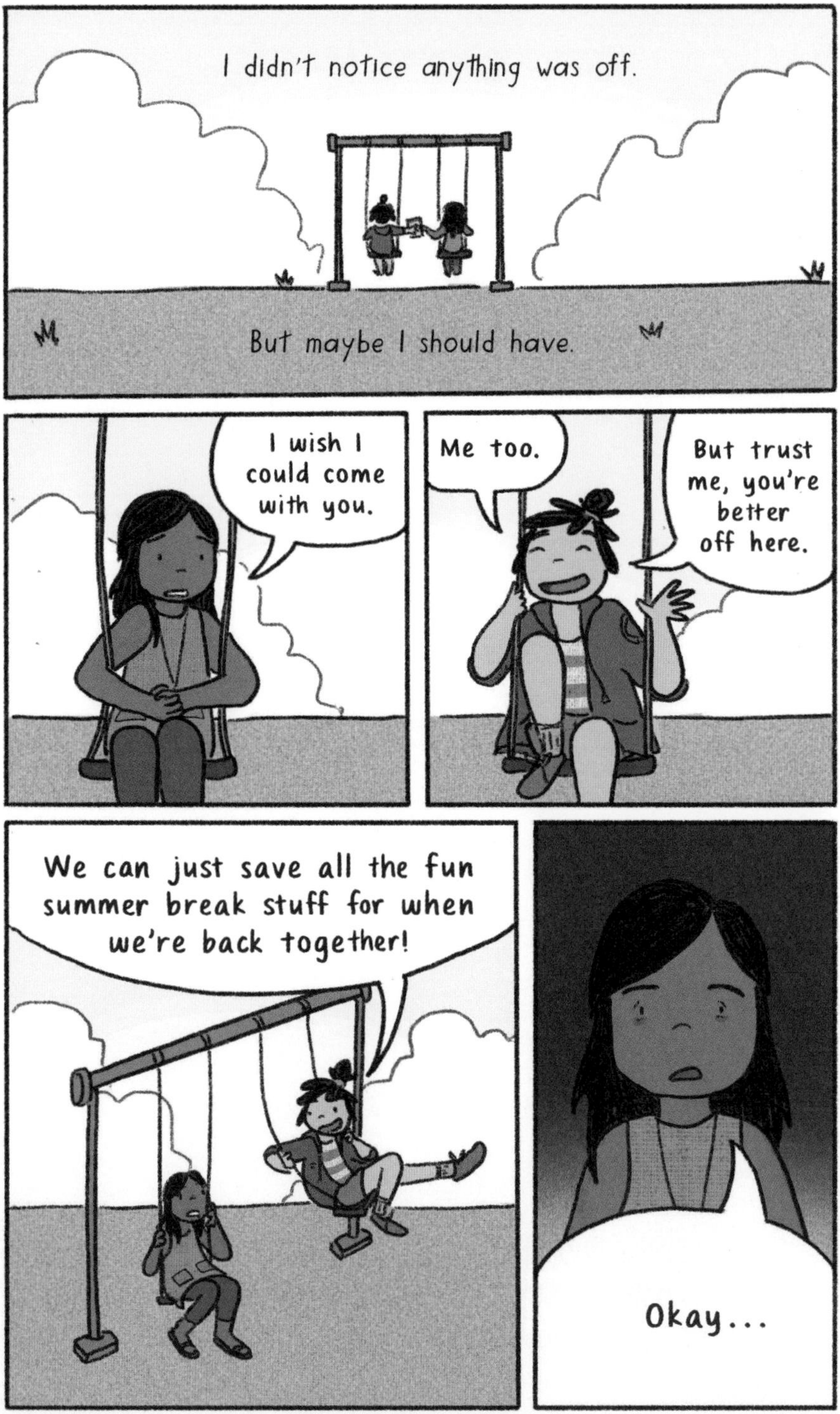
I didn't notice anything was off.
But maybe I should have.
I wish I could come with you.
Me too.
But trust me, you're better off here.
We can just save all the fun summer break stuff for when we're back together!
Okay...

I tried to send Nisha some updates while I was away, but the internet connection was horrible and I'm not sure any messages made it through.

I didn't hear from her at all!

Everything about this summer felt wrong somehow, but I figured it was just overheating and stress and being away from home.

I thought it would all be okay once I got back . . .

But it hasn't been.

CHAPTER 2

Even though I'm home now, something still doesn't feel right. Maybe I need time to adjust to regular life, like when you wake up from a nap feeling groggy and it takes a while to feel normal.

Mom and Dad seem happy to have me around again, but I can tell they've been really busy and are a little distracted.

They've been acting weirder than usual.

Sometimes they'll stop talking as soon as I walk into the room or stare at each other like they're communicating with their minds.

Maybe this is what happens when you leave your parents alone for too long. They don't know what to do with themselves!

The weirdest part, though, is Nisha.

Why hasn't she responded?

Is this thing broken?

I've been home for a few days already, and I haven't seen her once.

She still hasn't responded to my messages, and when I passed by her apartment earlier, it didn't look like anyone was home.

NISHA'S APARTMENT

I don't know where she could be!

It's been such a long time since we hung out, and we have SO MUCH to talk about.

I've been keeping track!

Summer is almost over and school is starting next week, so everyone is back in town, but Nisha doesn't seem to be among them. When I ask around, no one else has seen her either.

I spend a lot of time in our neighborhood—watching people and drawing what I see—so I thought I knew everything that went on around here.

But since I've been away, something has happened. Something *is happening*.

And I didn't see it coming.

CHAPTER 3

I don't usually get nervous about the first day of school, but I've never had to face it alone before. Nisha's always been there with me.

Every year before school started, we made a game plan and a pact.

BEST FRIENDS FOREVER!

BEST SCHOOL YEAR EVER!

That's how we always survived—together.

mapping out the best
path between classes

INCLUDES
STUFF LIKE...

KACIE & NISHA'S
5TH GRADE
SURVIVAL GUIDE

Kacie + Nisha's
4TH
GRADE
SURVIVAL
GUIDE

Kacie
+ Nisha's
3RD GRADE
SURVIVAL GUIDE

finding our
ideal lunch
spot

picking
a meeting
point for
the bus

But this year, I don't even know what classes she's in!

When I get to school, everyone is reuniting with their friends and catching up on what happened this summer.

But I'm on my own.

Nisha's not here and school just isn't the same without her.

Most people already have their usual groups, and I don't think we have a lot in common anyway.

It's okay, though. I'll just keep to myself and focus on my art until Nisha shows up— whenever that is.

Except everyone knows Nisha and I are best friends, so when people finally start noticing that she's not at school, they look to ME for answers . . .

Answers I don't even have!

Nisha and I used to say that we knew everything about each other.

But I guess that wasn't entirely true. I didn't know anything about *this*.

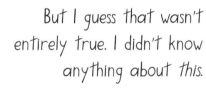

CHAPTER 4

Khanna's Grocery & Deli has been around for ages, and it's never changed much. Seeing the building boarded up and blocked off makes me nervous.

But who knows?

There could be a lot of reasons why Khanna's Grocery & Deli is under construction.

Maybe Mr. Khanna finally decided to remodel.

Or the freezers broke down and they had to close the store to replace them.

It could even be that they found a secret tunnel in the back room that leads to an undiscovered stash of buried treasure!

Whatever it is, something is changing, and I don't like not knowing what it is.

At least I don't have to worry about Smiley's Cleaners changing. My parents never change anything—even if they probably should.

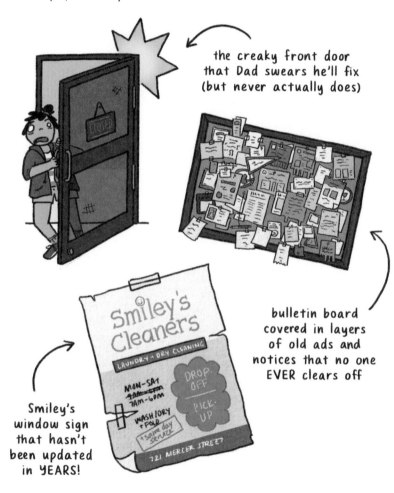

the creaky front door that Dad swears he'll fix (but never actually does)

bulletin board covered in layers of old ads and notices that no one EVER clears off

Smiley's window sign that hasn't been updated in YEARS!

They just never get around to it. I guess they ARE pretty busy.

When they're not driving around in our old van doing laundry pick-ups and drop-offs, they're stuck in the back office doing business stuff.

That's why they have Uncle Ott out front to handle the customers . . . and keep an eye on me.

Uncle Ott is not technically my uncle or even really related to me, but I've known him since I was born, so he's basically like family.

Uncle Ott always has something to say, and since we haven't had that many customers coming in lately, I'm usually the only one there to listen to him. When I ask if he knows anything about the construction down the street, he gets this look on his face like it's weird that I'm asking.

Don't know.

I just mind my own business.

You should try it.

his classic Uncle Ott eye twitch suggests otherwise

He says that a lot—especially when it comes to the drawings in my sketchbook.

Uncle Ott doesn't get it. He likes for things to be straightforward and useful (i.e., boring), and he doesn't see much use for art.

Plus, he thinks I should be careful about getting into other people's business.

But I'm an artist and I have to draw what I see!

Besides, my art helps me notice what other people don't, and *that* can be very useful.

Nisha was the one who helped me see that.

She was the kind of person who saw someone with a problem...

Give it! It's MY turn!

No, it's NOT! You just had it!

and wanted to help them solve it.

What about your sketchbook?

That's when we discovered how to use my drawings to help people around the neighborhood.

When we put all the right pieces together...

Truce!

we could figure out ANYTHING.

Like when Mrs. Acosta's community garden plot suffered a mysterious strawberry shortage...

What's going on?

Maya Acosta

we uncovered the sneaky (but adorable) culprit—her daughter.

Or when someone knocked over the library's entire summer reading display...

Now what do I do?

we knew exactly how to fix it and make it right again.

Oh no...

When Uncle Ott had a major mix-up with the laundry tags at Smiley's...

we used my notes and drawings to sort everything out.

No matter what the problem, we could solve it—TOGETHER.

We made the best team.

KACIE
THE PERCEPTIVE ARTIST!

NISHA
THE PEOPLE'S CHAMPION!

observing everything

collecting the clues

reaching out to others

connecting the dots

Nisha always said we couldn't do it without my drawings. But the truth is, I couldn't do it without *her*—only now I have to.

She may not be around, but I still have my sketchbooks.

Maybe they can help me figure out what happened to her.

Everyone in this neighborhood has a question they want answered or problem they need solved.

And now I guess, so do I.

CHAPTER 5

It's been a few days and Nisha still hasn't shown up at school, so I decide to start my investigations in the neighborhood.

My first stop is Deckled Edge, the used bookstore in town. Nisha and I spent many weekends huddled in the back corner reading comic books.

Ms. Davis owns Deckled Edge and always has the inside scoop on all the latest comic book issues, but apparently, she doesn't know anything about where Nisha might be. She can't even remember the last time Nisha was in the store!

I'm not surprised, though. Ms. Davis is not exactly known for having a great memory. She's constantly losing things!

I know I left my keys around here somewhere...

Nisha once told me that my sketchbooks carried a lot more information than I realized, that it was just a matter of figuring out how to use them.

MISSING
MS. DAVIS'S KEYS

If she were here, she'd offer to help Ms. Davis find her keys.

Now I guess
that's up to me.

You did it!
Brilliant!

Ms. Davis is so grateful that she lets me pick out any comic book I want as a reward! While I'm trying to decide, I overhear her talking to a customer about Nisha's store.

Did you see they're done renovating down the street?

Finally! That construction has been going on all summer...

Finally, some information I can use! I race down the street toward Khanna's Grocery & Deli. I've never run this fast before—so fast that I may have knocked over some people as I whooshed past.

If Nisha is not at the store, I know at least her dad will be. He practically lives there.

Mr. Khanna is always working.

Restocking shelves . . .

moving boxes in the back . . .

and helping customers find what they're looking for.

He'll know where she is.

But when I turn the corner, Khanna's is GONE. Not the building (that's still there), but everything else.

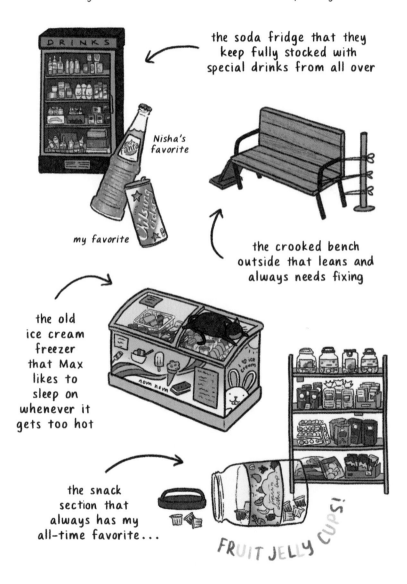

the soda fridge that they keep fully stocked with special drinks from all over

Nisha's favorite

my favorite

the crooked bench outside that leans and always needs fixing

the old ice cream freezer that Max likes to sleep on whenever it gets too hot

the snack section that always has my all-time favorite...

FRUIT JELLY CUPS!

The Khanna's Grocery & Deli I knew just isn't there anymore. In its place is something very, very different.

There are $Marts all over, but there's never been one on Mercer Street before.

What is it doing there? More importantly, what happened to Khanna's? It's like it has been totally erased from the block. If a stranger passed by now, they wouldn't know it ever existed. But I know.

Nisha's family owned that store for as long as I can remember. It couldn't have vanished for NO REASON . . . *She* couldn't have! There's only one thing to do: take a closer look at everything and find out what's really going on.

CHAPTER 6

By the time I get back to Smiley's, it's a lot later than usual. I know Uncle Ott won't snitch to my parents and get me in any real trouble, but he'll probably make me sit through one of his boring lectures about responsibility.

MARCUS

Lucky for me, he's in the middle of helping Marcus, one of our regular customers, so I slip right past him.

Marcus works at Mo's Diner, a restaurant nearby that's owned by (you guessed it) a guy named Mo.

Mom and Dad told me that Mo was one of their first customers when they started Smiley's Cleaners.

He's also our *best* customer!

Now Marcus is the one who comes by Smiley's at least once a week to drop off and pick up the restaurant's laundry.

Marcus is an artist too. We've never actually talked about it, but I can tell.

always has
pens + pencils

ink stains
on his hands

carries a little
sketchbook in
his back pocket
that looks like it
gets a *lot* of use

paint
on his
clothes

I wonder what he draws in his sketchbook . . .

He'd probably show me if I asked, but art can be a very personal thing and I don't think I'm ready to show him MY sketchbook yet either.

Marcus is usually really friendly and upbeat, but today he seems off. Uncle Ott notices too, and since he has no filter, he just says so.

Apparently things have been a bit rough for Marcus—at work and at home! Mo is in a bad mood because someone keeps changing the sign outside the restaurant to say *Moo's* Diner, and Marcus hasn't been getting much sleep lately.

As an artist, you always have to be in observation mode. That's how you pick up on important details—even the ones that don't seem important in the moment. Sometimes, those are the key to everything.

Uncle Ott hands Marcus his receipt and some spare earplugs he found in the back room. Marcus says thank you, puts on his headphones, and leaves.

It doesn't click until later.

There's something so familiar here.

It takes me a while...

but then I finally see it.

Now I remember...

Hey! I'm here!

Be right down!

Nisha and Marcus are NEIGHBORS.

Or at least they used to be...

mirabella
APARTMENTS

Where are the Khannas and who is in their apartment?

Up until now, I was hoping that maybe her family was just on a long vacation or something.

WAIT!!!

What about Nisha and her dad?!?!

Hmm... Actually, I dunno! I haven't seen them around lately.

This sounds permanent. But my best friend wouldn't leave *permanently* without telling me, would she?

I need to know for sure.

CHAPTER 7

One thing I've learned from my observations is that sometimes it takes time for interesting things to happen. You just have to make sure you're in the right place at the right time.

The next day after school, I find a spot across the street with a clear view of Nisha's apartment and wait.

NISHA'S APARTMENT BUILDING

good distance to observe but not seem like a stalker

MERCER STREET COMMUNITY GARDEN

me

I draw and I wait.

I wait and I dra

Eventually,
it pays off.

The mail is here, and a package gets delivered right to Nisha's apartment.

Before the door opens, there is a part of me that still believes she might be there . . .

even though I can hear a dog barking through the walls and I know Mr. Khanna is allergic to dogs.

Then a boy answers the door.

DEFINITELY *NOT* NISHA

I've never seen him before and I know *everybody* in town. Whoever he is, I don't trust him.

He takes the package and goes back into the apartment. *Nisha's apartment.*

When I get a closer look, I realize these *strangers* have changed everything. I have so many memories of Nisha's place, but I don't recognize it now.

It's like the Khannas never even lived there!

different-colored curtains

photos of strangers

some lady I've never seen before

a kid I don't know (+ his dog!)

fancy new couch

Last year, our class went on an epic overnight field trip.

Well, instead, why don't you do something special together?

So I spent the night at her apartment...

BFF SLEEPOVER!!!

HAHAHAHAHAHAHAHAHAHAHAHAH

and we made it pretty epic.

Considering how it all turned out, I think we actually had a better time than the rest of the class.

What happened?!?!

...FOOD...POISONING...

Suddenly, my stomach feels weirdly empty, but it isn't because I'm hungry. It's the same feeling I had when Nisha didn't respond to any of my emails and my text messages stopped going through.

 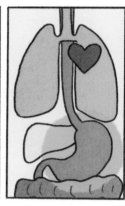 

It knows something is off.

Ms. Dascha delivers mail to the whole neighborhood.

MS. DASCHA RHODES

She talks to everyone, so she has access to a lot of information. She might not have a sketchbook like I do, but she doesn't need one. She keeps it all in her head. If anyone knows anything about Nisha's family, it's her.

Didn't they move away this summer? Went to live with family or something like that.

They're forwarding their mail to a new address...

I don't want her to be right, but my gut tells me she is. Nisha doesn't have a lot of family here.

Her closest relatives live super far away—a second cousin or great-aunt or something like that.

B-but, I don't get it. Why couldn't they just stay?

Ms. Dascha says she doesn't really know why they left, but she can't quite look me in the eye when she tells me that. Maybe she has some idea but doesn't want to say.

She still has a lot of mail to deliver, so she says goodbye and continues on her route through the neighborhood. I should probably go too. It's getting late, and there's not much more to look for here.

Part of being a great artist is seeing EVERYTHING—even things you don't necessarily want to see.

I have to face the facts.

Nisha is gone, and she probably isn't coming back.

CHAPTER 8

Even though Mom and Dad are always busy, they make sure we have dinner together every night.

It's tradition for us to eat and watch *Wheel of Fortune* together.

Dad isn't great at it, but Mom and I get *very* competitive. Except I'm not in the mood today.

Today, I'm trying to fill in the blanks of a totally different kind of puzzle.

They don't seem surprised, which makes me wonder if they somehow know more about it than I do.

My parents share a look.

It happens so fast that most people would miss it, but not me!

It's like they're saying something to each other without actually saying anything.

Well, sometimes things happen...

What does that mean?

What THINGS?

Just as I'm about to ask them what else they know, one of the contestants spins the wheel and lands on BANKRUPT.

SHERRILYN
a small business owner from Houston, Texas

BANKRUPT

Oh no! She'll never get that all back...

Wahhh! But she was doing so good...

What?!?! That's not fair!

We're all so focused on watching her try to recover from that bad spin that there is no more mention of Nisha or the Khanna family for the rest of the show.

In the end, Sherrilyn comes in second, and *Wheel of Fortune* is over. I want to bring up the Khannas again, but before I get the chance, Dad's phone rings.

Mr. S-s-see-sit-sith-something... um... *sir*?

This is Elaine from Mercer Street Bank calling in regards to your loan...

My parents disappear into the other room to take the call and leave me to clean up.

Clear the table and then go do your homework, okay?

It's totally unfair.

...

Besides, I can't focus on homework when I'm still trying to make sense of what I learned today.

Nisha didn't vanish—
she moved away.

I should be relieved to know the truth, but I still feel like I'm missing something. I'm not sure what answers I'm looking for now, but the questions only seem to be getting more complicated.

Later that evening, Mom comes in to check on me. I try to bring up Nisha again, but she just changes the subject.

Now that I think about it, a lot of grown-ups have been acting weird lately—and not just when I ask about Nisha.

It's like there's something they don't want kids to know or think we won't be able to understand.

But I notice a lot more than they think I do.

I have a feeling that if I want to get to the bottom of why Nisha left, I'll have to figure it out for myself.

CHAPTER 9

Since asking questions isn't getting me very far, I decide to take a more strategic approach.

The good thing about being a neighborhood kid is that everyone is used to seeing you around. Grown-ups don't think twice about you or pay much attention to what you're up to.

This makes it easier to notice what people are up to without seeming suspicious.

Maybe if I hang around $Mart long enough, I'll find out why it's there and what happened to Khanna's Grocery & Deli.

It's $Mart's grand opening, and they've made sure Mercer Street knows it.

It's all so new and flashy, but not everybody seems impressed by it.

Mo rolls his eyes and goes back into the diner.

Ms. Davis frowns as she walks past all the $Mart promotions and promoters taking over the sidewalk.

Mrs. Acosta's kid won't stop crying!

In front of the store, I spy a man in a fancy suit talking to a reporter. The Suit seems important, so I stand close enough to listen to their conversation.

He makes this sound like a good thing, but I'm not so sure it is.

For a while, he welcomes people into the store and poses for photos. His smile is all stiff and plastic— the kind that you're forced to hold when you take class pictures.

I try to sneak by unnoticed, but get pulled into a photo even though I hate taking them!

As soon as the reporter leaves, the Suit stops smiling, walks to his fancy car, and zooms away. He doesn't look back.

CHAPTER 10

The more time I spend in $Mart, the more it feels out of place on this corner of Mercer Street. The building might be the same, but something about $Mart just doesn't fit.

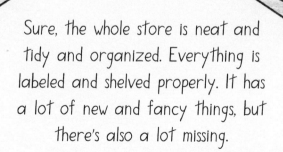

Sure, the whole store is neat and tidy and organized. Everything is labeled and shelved properly. It has a lot of new and fancy things, but there's also a lot missing.

Where is the deli station that serves the best bacon, egg, and cheese sandwiches?

Or the counter by the window where people sit around to chat about their day?

Or the small, clunky TV that Mr. Khanna installed so he wouldn't have to miss any World Cup matches?

Khanna's Grocery & Deli was a little cluttered and chaotic, but Mr. Khanna always made sure to have what we needed.

Now that $Mart has changed everything, being here makes me feel like *I'm* the one that's out of place.

Like *I'm* the one that doesn't fit.

For a while, I wander around the store feeling a little lost until I end up in the frozen food section and overhear Mrs. Acosta and Ms. Davis talking in the next aisle.

...different.

Well, it's new and definitely something...

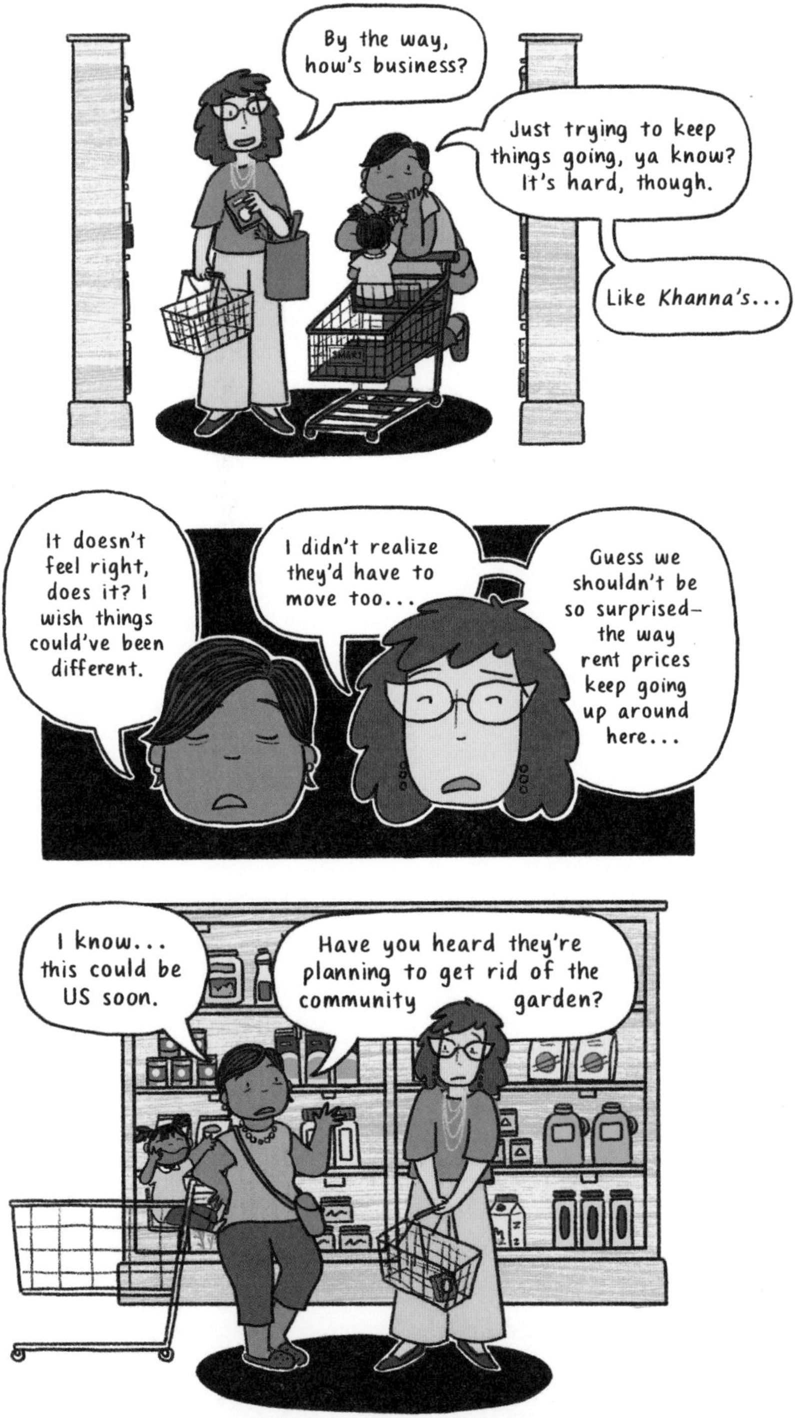
By the way, how's business?
Just trying to keep things going, ya know? It's hard, though.
Like Khanna's...
It doesn't feel right, does it? I wish things could've been different.
I didn't realize they'd have to move too...
Guess we shouldn't be so surprised— the way rent prices keep going up around here...
I know... this could be US soon.
Have you heard they're planning to get rid of the community garden?

A sharp voice breaks through their conversation, and I turn to see the store manager yelling at me.

HEY, YOU!

WHERE ARE YOUR PARENTS?

At first, I don't realize she's talking to me. Everyone in the neighborhood knows my parents own Smiley's Cleaners and are busy working right now, but I guess the $Mart Manager Lady isn't from around here.

She looks like her head is about to explode,
so I ask for help to distract her.

But then she gives me
a weird look, like
I'm playing some
kind of trick.

Turns out, she's
not much help!

I know that's my cue to leave, and I can feel her watching me as I exit.

When I make it outside, I can finally breathe again.

I don't think I want to spend any more time here.

There's no reason to anymore.

It finally hits me that $Mart being here means Khanna's Grocery & Deli *isn't*. I used to think of it as my best friend's family store—somewhere we used to go just because it was . . . there.

Nisha and I spent a lot of hours in Khanna's Grocery & Deli.

Usually we just hung around...

...watching customers...

...and wasting time.

Sometimes, Mr. Khanna asked us to help out with the store.

It was kind of strange.

I never liked having to help my parents at Smiley's...

But Mr. Khanna could be very convincing.

How about one of every flavor— EACH?

Then, together, Nisha and I found a way to make it fun.

LET'S DO THIS!

Good work, you two!

Maybe it's easier to notice how important things are when they're not around. I never thought Khanna's Grocery & Deli was the kind of place I'd miss . . .

But now that it's gone for good, I'm not sure what I'll do without it.

CHAPTER 11

It's been almost TWO WEEKS since I found out Nisha was gone. But just when I think I've accepted the fact that she moved away, I come across something I didn't see before, and it brings up all these other questions that seem so much bigger than us.

It's kind of like pulling on a loose thread, only to realize you're unraveling a giant hole in your sweater.

At some point, the only thing to do is keep following it.

I can't stop thinking about the conversation I overheard at $Mart. I've learned a lot from secretly observing adults in the neighborhood, but I can tell I'm still missing something. At least I know where to go next.

The community garden is right across the street from Nisha's place, so I walk past it all the time.

Nisha used to have her own plot there, though I'm not sure what's happened to it now.

She always asked me to help, but I decided early on that gardening was too messy for me.

Nisha never minded that though.

I remember her crouching down in the dirt to take care of new sprouts and whispering nice things as she watered them. She had a knack for growing things.

I wonder how her plants are doing without her around, but before I get the chance to check on them, someone unexpected blocks my path.

I've never seen anybody wear an expensive suit in the community garden, but my gut tells me he and his friend aren't exactly there to plant things.

They lurk around the plots and planters, pointing to stuff and snapping photos and taking notes. I crouch by a patch of tomatoes and pretend to be inspecting the vines while I eavesdrop.

I try my best to go unnoticed, but eventually, they see me.

For a second, I think he recognizes me from the $Mart grand opening last week. He doesn't. He thinks I'm some random kid who will listen to him brag about his plan for the neighborhood.

I know adults, so I know what he *wants* me to say. But the truth is, we don't need it.

Besides, I like what's already here.

Before I get a chance to tell him that, Mrs. Acosta and Ms. Davis come rushing over.

They don't look very happy.

Why don't you take Maya and go water the strawberries while us grown-ups talk?

I'd rather stay close so I can hear what they're saying, but Mrs. Acosta's strawberry patch is all the way on the other side of the garden and watching Maya requires my full attention.

By the time I finish watering the strawberries and wrangling Maya, the Suit and his friend are gone.

Mrs. Acosta and Ms. Davis don't say much after that. Not to me.

They just give each other *looks*, but luckily, I'm getting better at figuring out what these grown-up looks mean. Something is happening to Mercer Street, and even the adults don't seem to know what to do about it.

What if Khanna's Grocery & Deli isn't the only thing that's changing around here?

If what the Suit said is true, soon the whole neighborhood could be totally different. And then maybe it won't be just Nisha and her plants I have to worry about.

CHAPTER 12

When you need to think, there is no better place than on the swings. It is an unspoken fact that the swings are the best part of any park.

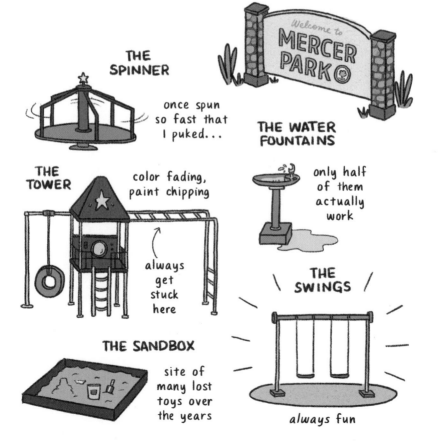

THE SPINNER

once spun so fast that I puked...

Welcome to MERCER PARK

THE WATER FOUNTAINS

only half of them actually work

THE TOWER

color fading, paint chipping

always get stuck here

THE SANDBOX

site of many lost toys over the years

THE SWINGS

always fun

Whenever we went to Mercer Park, Nisha and I always staked our claim on the swings. Now they've been taken over by some neighborhood kids a few years younger than us.

I guess it's fine.

Without Nisha around, the swings don't totally feel like ours anyway.

Instead, I plop down on a bench and open up my sketchbook. Usually when I draw, everything else fades away, but right now, I can't seem to focus. Everything feels so complicated—even art.

MR. BECKER

BENCH GRANDPAS

MR. XIN

The Bench Grandpas are as much a part of the park as the swings. They're always there . . .

playing chess . . .

bickering about whatever golf tournament is going on that week . . .

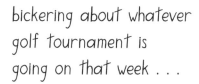

and snacking on sunflower seeds and root beer.

They've been part of this neighborhood since before it was even a real neighborhood. At least, that's what they say.

The Bench Grandpas like to talk. A LOT.

Back in the day, I was the county's championship ballroom dancer five years in a row! You should've seen me move!

Well, before everyone had a cell phone, we left each other paper notes around town. But on a windy or rainy day? Forget it.

That summer, everyone thought the Mercer Street movie theater was haunted... But it was just me messing with the lights on my lunch break!

Admit it! You thought he trained that evil squirrel to torture you! I wonder what happened to it...

There used to be a nice old lady who came around on Tuesdays with a cart of fresh pastries. I miss those croissants!

I'm telling ya, that coin was one of a kind! And if he hadn't "accidentally" dropped it in the river that day, I'd definitely be a millionaire.

But they also happen to be very good listeners. They have a way of getting you to admit things you might not even be ready to admit to yourself.

As soon as I start telling them what happened at $Mart, the rest of the story comes pouring out.

BUT WHY IS THIS EVEN HAPPENING? WHY IS EVERYTHING CHANGING?!?/ I HATE IT.

When I finish, they sigh and give each other a *look*, but there's something different about it that I'm not used to seeing—like they have a lot to say, but aren't sure where to start.

I don't know if there's even an actual answer or if this is one of those hypothetical questions that's supposed to teach you something about the world.

Before they can say more, a loud grinding noise suddenly catches our attention.

There's a boy doing skateboard tricks off one of the park benches! He must not be from around here because the whole neighborhood knows that the park is Bench Grandpa territory.

They do NOT tolerate littering, vandalism, or anyone messing with park property.

THIS IS A PUBLIC PARK!

HEY, YOU! STOP THAT!

And they will certainly let you know it.

Skateboard Boy might not be a Mercer Street neighborhood kid, but he does look oddly familiar. Then it hits me. I've seen him before . . .

He's the boy in Nisha's apartment!

First he and his noisy dog take over Nisha's home. Now he's trying to take over *our* park with his noisy skateboarding?

Who does he think he is?

When he finally realizes we're all yelling at *him*, he loses his balance and the skateboard goes flying.

I almost feel bad for him because he falls right on his butt, and park concrete is NOT a great place to land. When he gets up, he looks embarrassed, but I'm not sure if it's from falling or from getting in trouble. Maybe both.

He yelps out a quick apology, picks up his skateboard, and scurries away. He seems a little rattled.

SORRY!!!

He doesn't know that even though the Bench Grandpas try to be scary, they're mostly harmless. The Bench Grandpas are kind of like Mercer Street's guardians—the original observers.

They keep watch over the park and make note of everything that happens in the neighborhood. So did they see these changes coming? Can they see what's next? I'm not sure it matters either way. There's not much anyone can do about it.

If there were, Nisha might still be here.

CHAPTER 13

I don't particularly want to see more of Skateboard Boy around the neighborhood, but it's like I can't get rid of him!

On my way back to Smiley's, there he is again, only this time, he's outside the diner being yelled at by Mo.

You've got some nerve messing with my diner!

I can't help but feel bad for him. Unlike the Bench Grandpas, when Mo is trying to be scary, he really means it.

Whoever messed up Mo's sign a couple of weeks ago has decided to take it a step further. The whole side of the building is marked up!

And Skateboard Boy is right there, holding a can of spray paint.

IT WASN'T ME!!!

I just found it over there and was gonna use it to touch up my board...

I DON'T EVEN KNOW HOW TO DRAW A COW!

I see why Mo thinks he's guilty . . .

But I know for a fact that he's NOT, and I could probably help prove it.

There's a part of me that doesn't want to help him—the part that would rather just blame him for Nisha moving away, for taking her place, for being somewhere he doesn't belong. For a second, I consider walking away and leaving him to figure this all out for himself.

But then I think about Nisha.

When I was new to the neighborhood, she welcomed me and showed me around. She made Mercer Street feel like it could be *home*, and eventually, it WAS.

C'mon! Go help!

If she were here, I know she'd help him.

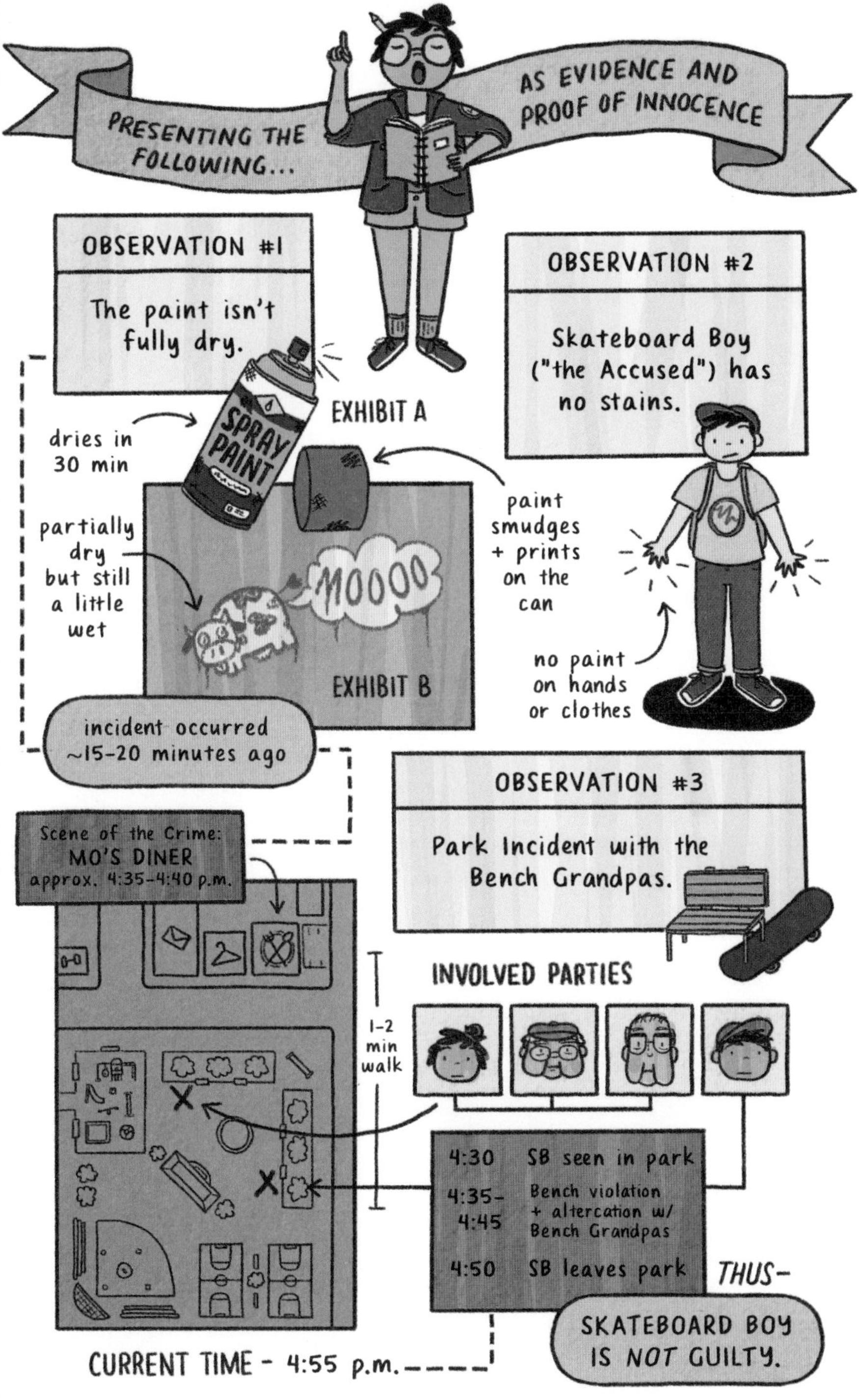
PRESENTING THE FOLLOWING...
AS EVIDENCE AND PROOF OF INNOCENCE
OBSERVATION #1
The paint isn't fully dry.
OBSERVATION #2
Skateboard Boy ("the Accused") has no stains.
dries in 30 min
SPRAY PAINT
EXHIBIT A
paint smudges + prints on the can
partially dry but still a little wet
MOOOO
EXHIBIT B
no paint on hands or clothes
incident occurred ~15-20 minutes ago
OBSERVATION #3
Park Incident with the Bench Grandpas.
Scene of the Crime: MO'S DINER approx. 4:35-4:40 p.m.
INVOLVED PARTIES
1-2 min walk
4:30 SB seen in park
4:35-4:45 Bench violation + altercation w/ Bench Grandpas
4:50 SB leaves park
THUS-
SKATEBOARD BOY IS NOT GUILTY.
CURRENT TIME - 4:55 p.m.

After I've made my case, Mo finally admits that he probably has the wrong person.

Okay, fine then.

But stay outta trouble and keep an eye out for me.

He still seems a little suspicious though, and I can understand why.

Mo is one of the nicest adults I know, but it takes him a while to warm up to new people. I can be the same way.

At first, I saw Skateboard Boy as a stranger trying to replace Nisha and mess things up around town, but when I take another look, I think he might just be a kid who feels out of place and needs someone to give him a chance . . . which I guess is up to me.

Hi, I'm Kacie!

The first thing I learn is that
Skateboard Boy's real name is . . .

DANNY SOHN
"Skateboard Boy"

He moved to town with his mom a month ago, which
explains a lot. There are certain things that every
neighborhood kid knows, and he doesn't seem to know
ANY of them.

He turned his family's
hardware store into a
barber shop
and salon,
but kept the
old sign!

HALL + HALL

Squirrels invaded the
bathroom and it's
been out of order
ever since. They might
still be in there...

At closing
time, they
give out
the leftover
pastries so
they don't go
to waste.

Forget it.
The bus NEVER
stops here.
It's cursed!

When we pass by Viva Paletas, it becomes even more clear that this kid needs major guidance.

I've never had one of those before!

WHAAAAAT?!?!

This is no ordinary Popsicle stand.

Mrs. Acosta makes her paletas from scratch with fresh fruit and herbs from the community garden. Maybe that's what makes Viva Paletas so special. I know that when Danny tries one, he'll understand.

He calls me his friend so easily, even though we only just met!

Are we? I don't know. Maybe we could be.

Still, it feels weird being here, eating paletas with Danny instead of Nisha.

This used to be our thing.

Well, Nisha and I were best friends, so EVERYTHING was kind of our thing.

I never had a best friend before Nisha.

As an only child, I spent a lot of time playing on my own.

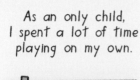

SMILEY'S CLEANERS

But when my parents moved to town and opened Smiley's, I started spending more time on Mercer Street.

Hi!

That's how I met Nisha.

Nisha had lived her whole life on Mercer Street.

She knew her way around the neighborhood.

She talked to everybody and was a part of everything.

When we finally became friends,  she made me feel like I was a part of everything too.

I thought it would always be like that.

KACIE AND NISHA, TAKING ON THE WORLD!

We can carpool to school together...

Take all the same classes...

Buy houses next door...

Get lockers next to each other...

Be roommates in college...

And basically hang out all the time!

Best friends, TOGETHER FOREVER!

KHANNA'S

CHAPTER 14

Ever since Nisha left, I've been keeping to myself and focusing on my drawings, hoping to find something in them that will help it all make sense.

Even at school, I spend most of my lunch period alone with my sketchbook.

But things are different with Danny around.

We may not have the same classes, but he always says hi when we see each other in the halls, and we've even started eating lunch together!

I don't get as much drawing done as I used to, but Danny always shares whatever extra food his mom packs him, so I don't mind too much.

Plus, he's kind of fun to have around.

Maybe this means we're becoming friends. I don't know though. I've never had many friends besides Nisha, and I'm not sure I know how to make new ones.

Danny and I don't have very much in common.

He loves skateboarding and I've never even tried it before.

I like art and Danny is more into music.

I spend most of my time watching people and noticing things, but Danny lives in his own world and doesn't always pay attention to what's going on around him.

It sometimes gets him into trouble.

When you think about it, we don't really make sense, but maybe being friends isn't just about liking the same stuff or looking at life the same way.

Maybe it's more about meeting someone where they're at.

I don't know anything about skateboarding, but I know this neighborhood and I think I can help Danny find what he's looking for.

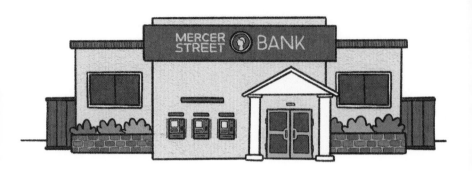

Mercer Street Bank is on the far side of town and has a parking lot in the back that no one pays much attention to. Over the years, it's become the unofficial hang out spot for any neighborhood kid who bikes or boards or skates.

I don't do any of that stuff, so I've never spent any time here, but I know it's exactly what Danny needs.

PERFECT!

At first, I sit off to the side, drawing in my notebook and watching Danny practice his tricks . . . until he makes it his mission to teach ME how to skateboard.

Danny is pretty different from Nisha, but right at that moment, he reminds me of her.

Nisha always wanted me to try new things.

Maybe that's why I agree to do it and end up standing on this wobbly board on wheels,

Even though I fall down
a few times . . .

(most of the time)

. . . I finally manage to make it
from one side of the parking lot
to the other, all on my own.

I'm not going to
become a professional
skateboarder any time
soon, but it felt like
progress. More than that,
it was actually fun.

WOO-
HOO!

I guess life can be kind of unexpected sometimes . . .

in good
ways . . .

. . . and bad.

As we leave the parking lot to head back home, something catches my eye—the Smiley's van parked on the street in front of us!

I don't see my parents, but I can guess where they might be. I have a gut feeling that something is up, but I'm just not sure what.

Nisha moving away has taught me that, whether you see it at first or not, there is always more going on with people than you think. I may have missed the signs before, but I won't let that happen again. This time, I'm going to find out what's happening.

CHAPTER 15

For a while, Danny and I wait by the van, watching people go in and out of the bank.

But he never asks why we're waiting.

Even though Danny and I haven't known each other for very long, I think he can sense that I don't want to talk about it.

Instead, he asks me to tell him more about the neighborhood, so I do.

I get so caught up in stories about Mercer Street that I almost forget why we're waiting here.

I don't even realize how much time has passed until Danny has to leave.

Sorry, but I gotta head home!

See ya later!

Then it's just me, alone with my sketchbook.

But I don't feel like drawing much.

I always thought that being an artist made me more aware of the world, but for all the sketchbooks I've filled and observations I've made, there's so much I still don't *get*.

Maybe it's not enough just to draw what I see. Maybe it takes a little more work to really understand what's going on.

Yes! My first paycheck!

What do I think I know?

My poor puppy...

So many unexpected fees!

What are they feeling?

What is really going on?

What might be harder to see?

Eventually, my parents come out of the bank, and I can tell that something is wrong. They're wearing stuffy clothes they usually never wear and are moving with a slow heaviness I've never really seen. They look so out of place.

More than that, they look upset . . .

. . . so upset
that they
don't even
see me
waiting by
the van.

My parents usually
never fight in front of me.

Whenever things get too tense, they share a look and go into another room. But the walls in our apartment are pretty thin and sometimes I can hear them arguing. It's always about boring things like bills or the business or which brand of soap saves us the most money. I don't pay too much attention to it.

But this time, it's happening right in front of me.

As soon as they notice me, they stop and act like nothing's wrong.

I want to pretend like I didn't see anything . . . but I *did.*

WHAT'S GOING ON?!?!

Your mom and I had to handle some business here today...

Don't worry! It's just grown-up stuff.

The truth is, I AM worried. How could I not be?

Ugh! I may not know exactly what's going on, but I do know what it means when they say it's "just grown-up stuff."

I *know* grown-up stuff. It shakes up the neighborhood and gets adults all nervous. It's messy and difficult and takes over everything.

Grown-up stuff means trouble . . .

for the old flower shop that used to be next door, for Khanna's Grocery & Deli, for the community garden, for who knows what else.

I think what they really want to say is that whatever is going on is not my business or is too complicated or won't matter to me because I'm *just a kid.*

Adults think every major problem is grown-up stuff.

But it's MY problem too.

One way or another, grown-up stuff is the reason why my best friend isn't around anymore. And I'm tired of not knowing anything about it.

I've never yelled like this before. When things make me angry, I usually keep them to myself or vent to Nisha. But now all the feelings I've been having lately are pushing their way to the surface, and I can't keep them inside anymore!

Honestly, I'm not just mad at my parents—
I'm mad at EVERYTHING and EVERYONE!

I'm mad at Nisha.
Mad at the $Mart people.
Mad at *myself*.

Mad that I didn't see what was happening right in front of me. Mad that, even if I *had*, there wasn't anything I could do about Nisha leaving.

I'm mad that everything around me is changing, but I'm just a kid so all I can do is draw pictures and watch it happen.

CHAPTER 16

I don't understand parents, and I don't think they understand us. Sometimes it seems impossible to talk to them. Nisha and I have a theory that our parents are friends because they are basically the same.

MY PARENTS

NISHA'S DAD

work nonstop

only buy stuff on sale

NEVER EXPLAIN ANYTHING!

Most of the time, they make decisions and expect us to just go along with them.

It feels like I'm never on the same page as they are or even allowed to read the same book.

Even though Nisha and her dad didn't always see eye to eye, they never really fought. Well, except this ONCE. I didn't think much of it when it happened last June. But now I wonder if there was more to it than I thought.

That day, Nisha showed up at my house unexpectedly.

She was really upset.

Can I stay here with you?

I'd never seen her like that before.

She didn't say exactly what the fight was about...

HE'S RUINING MY LIFE!

IT'S NOT FAIR!

but I could tell it was a big one.

I knew something was wrong.

But I didn't know how to ask.

She stayed over that night,

but the next day, her dad came to take her home.

I thought he'd be mad...

Nisha...

and that she'd be in trouble.

We have to go.

But when it came time to leave...

...

Bye...

they both just seemed...

kind of sad.

We never talked about it after that.

I'm not sure we knew how to.

Did Nisha know she was moving?
Why couldn't she tell me?
Why wouldn't she want to?

*I thought best friends knew
everything about each other . . .*

I want someone else to blame, and my parents happen
to be right there, telling me what to do without
really telling me ANYTHING.

So I pout and refuse
to talk during the
drive, which doesn't
seem to bother
them as much
as I want it to.
I'm not surprised.
That's just how
they are.

I know my parents. If something is wrong,
they'll just try to ignore it and go about
their day as if everything is fine.

But just when I think we're about to make the usual turn toward Smiley's . . . we go another way.

The thing is, our family doesn't go out to eat much. I've asked why before, but my parents never give me a very good answer.

The one exception is our monthly dinner at Mo's. On the last Friday of every month, Smiley's Cleaners closes early and we head over to Mo's Diner. I want to eat out more, so I'm always trying to get my parents to bend the rules, but they NEVER do.

Until *now.*

I can't help but wonder if they've been abducted and replaced by very convincing imposters.

Huh? But it's not the end of the month yet!

It's been a tough few weeks. I think maybe we can make an exception!

My parents are usually so predictable. They like to stick to the same routines, and I always know what to expect from them.

But here we are, at Mo's Diner on a completely random night in the middle of the month! I might as well do something unexpected, too.

They share that *look*—the one that usually means there's something they aren't saying to me. But even THAT doesn't seem to mean what I thought it did.

Because this time . . . we *talk*.

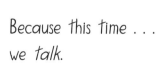

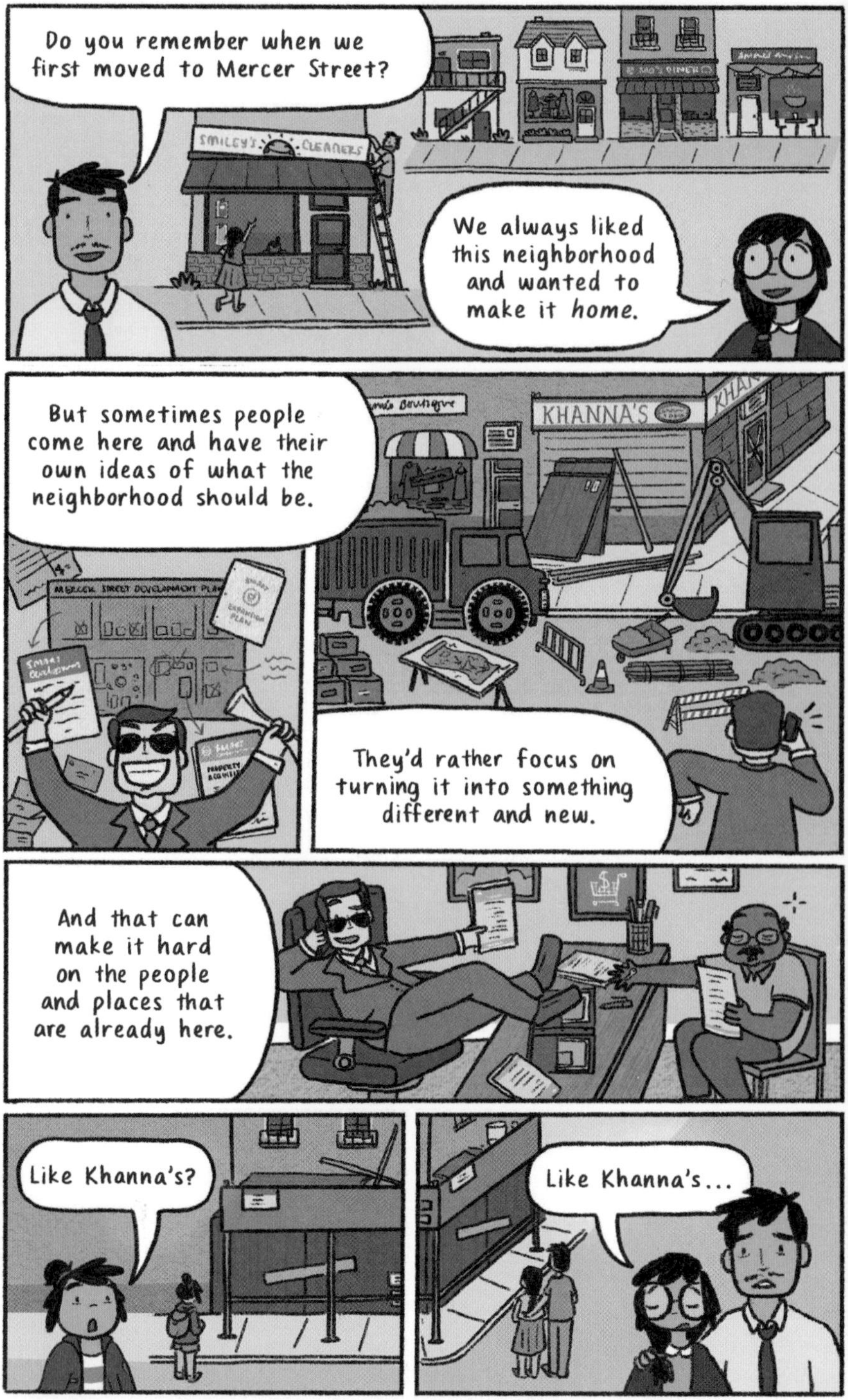
Do you remember when we first moved to Mercer Street?
SMILEY'S CLEANERS
We always liked this neighborhood and wanted to make it *home*.
But sometimes people come here and have their own ideas of what the neighborhood should be.
KHANNA'S
MERCER STREET DEVELOPMENT PLAN
They'd rather focus on turning it into something different and new.
And that can make it hard on the people and places that are already here.
Like Khanna's?
Like Khanna's...

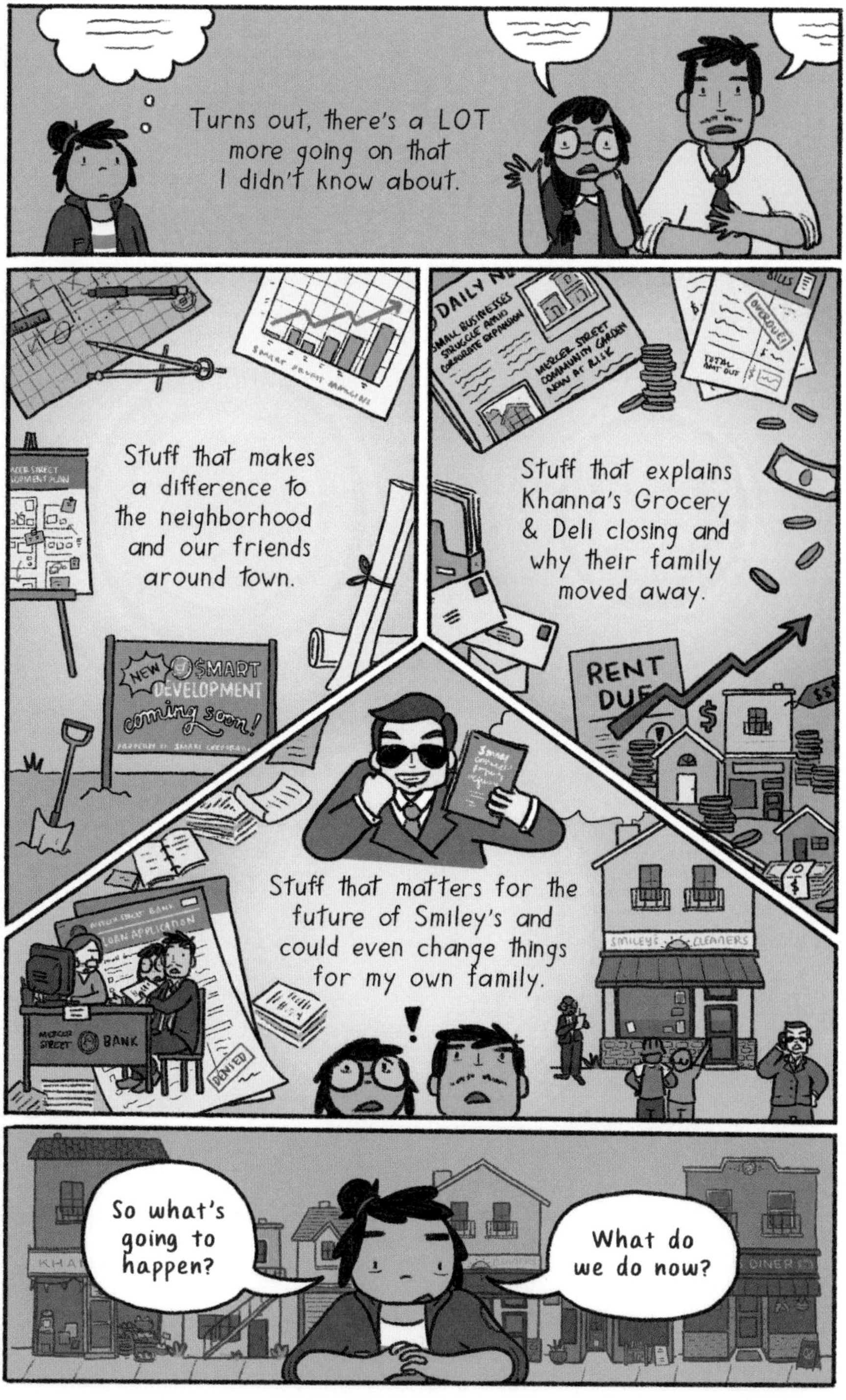

Turns out, there's a LOT more going on that I didn't know about.
SMALL BUSINESSES STRUGGLE AMID CORPORATE EXPANSION
MERCER STREET COMMUNITY GARDEN NOW AT RISK
BILLS
OVERDUE!
Stuff that makes a difference to the neighborhood and our friends around town.
Stuff that explains Khanna's Grocery & Deli closing and why their family moved away.
NEW
$MART DEVELOPMENT
coming soon!
RENT
LOAN APPLICATION
MERCER STREET BANK
DENIED
Stuff that matters for the future of Smiley's and could even change things for my own family.
SMILEY'S CLEANERS
!
So what's going to happen?
What do we do now?

Even though talking won't change what's happening, it *does* help me see things a little clearer.

Especially the complicated things.

They may be hard to talk about and hard to understand, but at least now I don't have to pretend like nothing is wrong.

CHAPTER 17

I think I understand my parents better now.

Mom says that sometimes, when things feel too big and complicated, it seems easier NOT to talk about them. Maybe that's how Nisha felt about leaving. Maybe it was easier to pretend like it wasn't happening.

After our family dinner at Mo's, I feel that way too. Part of me wants to forget everything—that the world is changing and that life is complicated and that my best friend is really gone.

But what good would it do?

Things HAVE changed. . .

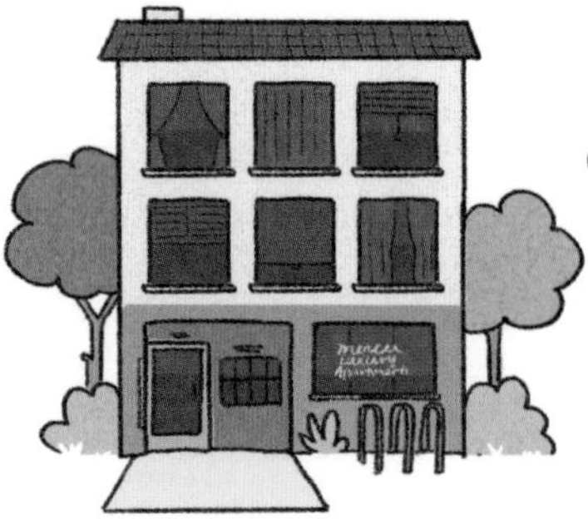

I've even been around to see some of it happen.

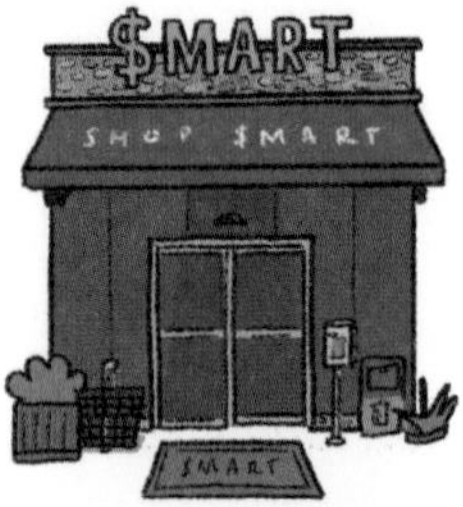
$MART
SHOP $MART

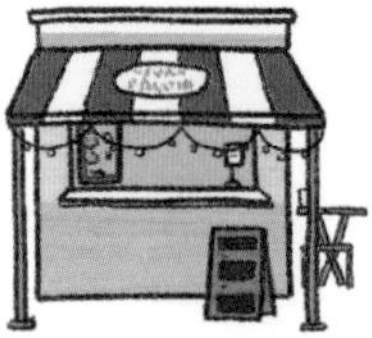

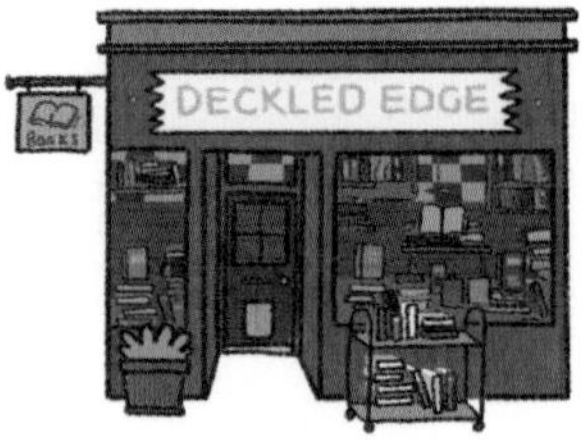
DECKLED EDGE
BOOKS

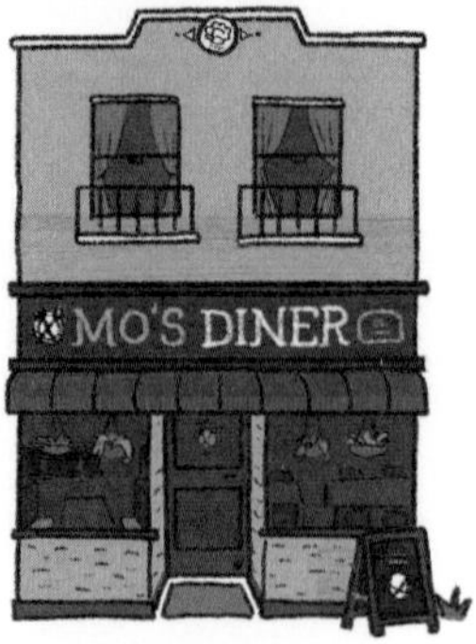
MO'S DINER

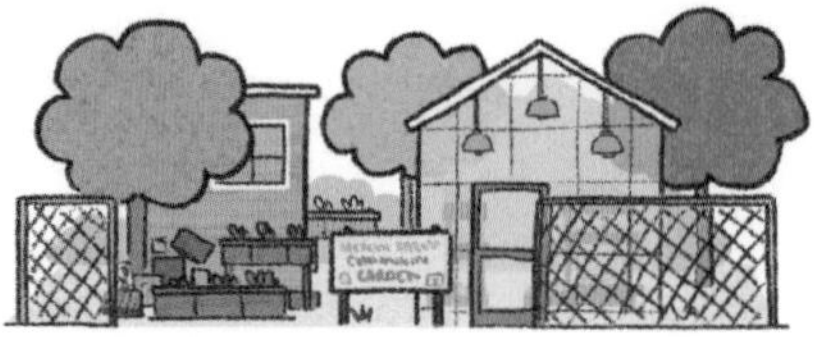

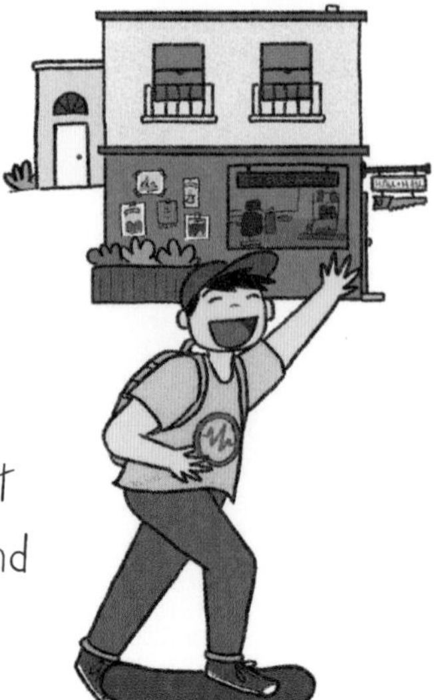

Whenever I spot Danny cruising down Mercer Street on his skateboard, I almost forget that he's new to the neighborhood and still discovering it for himself.

He doesn't know that the community garden used to be an abandoned dirt lot or that the $Mart on the corner used to be Khanna's Grocery & Deli or that my best friend, Nisha, used to live in the apartment he's living in now.

So much has changed.
So much is changing.

I'm starting to think of Danny less as Skateboard Boy and more as a real friend, and that's something new too.

It reminds me of what the Bench Grandpas say about change being part of life.

They've been around much MUCH longer than I have, and sometimes they talk about what it was like in "the old days."

Before Nisha and I met, before my family moved to town, before I was even born!

According to them, Smiley's Cleaners used to be a Chinese fast-food restaurant.

GOLDEN DRAGON
TO GO

Before Deckled Edge opened up, that building belonged to an old family accounting firm.

Mrs. Acosta used to work at the grocery store down the street and made paletas out of her kitchen for all the neighborhood kids.

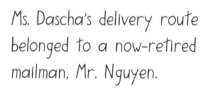

Ms. Dascha's delivery route belonged to a now-retired mailman, Mr. Nguyen.

At one point, Nisha's apartment complex didn't even exist!

I guess change happens whether we choose to notice it or not. And sometimes it's not what we expect.

Not everything that's changing is good,
but not all of it is bad either.

I think I just want
to know what will
change next and if
there's anything I
can do about it.

When I show my parents the poster I made, I expect them to just put it up on the bulletin board or something. But instead, they want to make copies and put them up all over the neighborhood for everyone to see!

I'm not sure I'm ready for that.

Everyone around town has seen me with my sketchbook, but they haven't seen what's inside. I don't show my art to many people.

What if they think it's silly or bad? What if they don't take me seriously? What if they say I'm not a real artist? What if they're right?

Surprisingly, even Uncle Ott thinks it's a good idea. He never seemed to think much of my drawings or care about art before.

He says he still doesn't get it, but maybe that can change.

It just goes to show that no matter how much you think you know about someone, they can still surprise you. And if Uncle Ott can change the way he sees things, so can I.

Sometimes one big thing happens that shifts the way you look at the people and places around you.

I need some help...
Meet me on Mercer Street?
OK!

Other times, that change happens little by little.

Keeping a sketchbook taught me to notice things, but now I know it takes a little more work to look closer and really *see* what's going on.

SIGN THE PETITION
MERCER STREET COMMUNITY GARDEN
SAVE OUR GARDEN
PROTECT COMMUNITY SPACES!

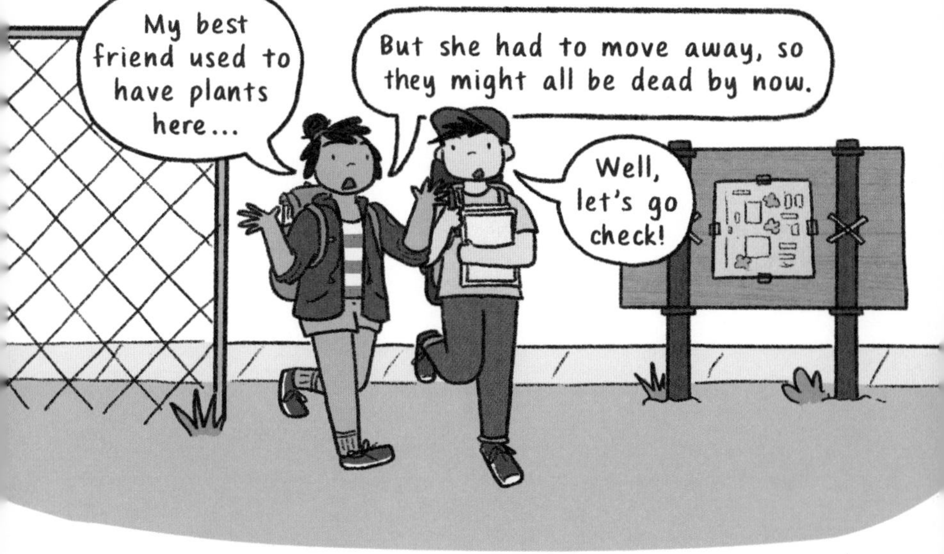
My best friend used to have plants here...
But she had to move away, so they might all be dead by now.
Well, let's go check!

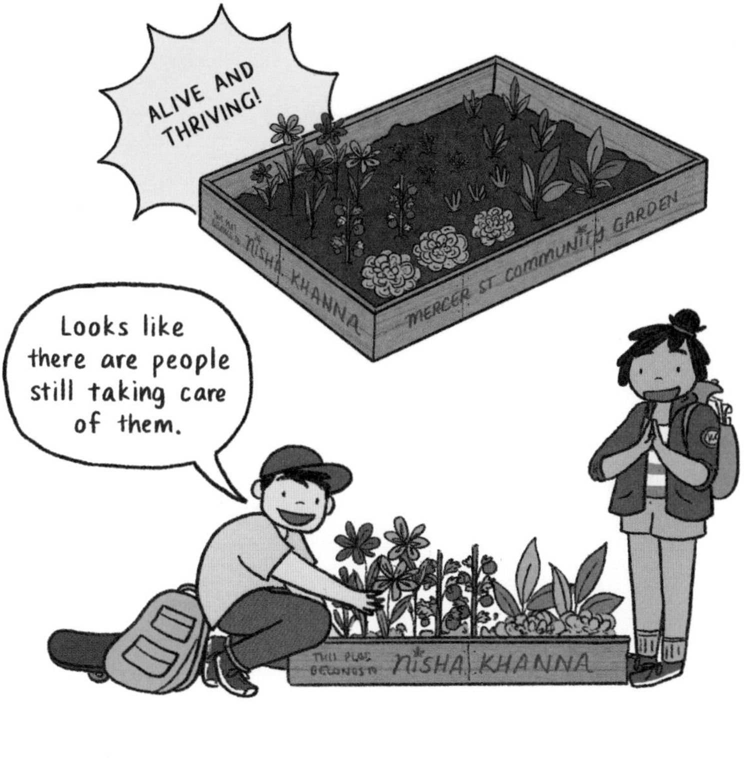
ALIVE AND THRIVING!
NISHA KHANNA
MERCER ST COMMUNITY GARDEN
Looks like there are people still taking care of them.
NISHA KHANNA

CHAPTER 18

It turns out everyone on Mercer Street has been pretty busy lately.

Mrs. Acosta and Ms. Davis are organizing a block party to raise money for the community garden. There's a lot to do, and they can't do it all alone.

C'mon! Let's go help!

I may be a kid, but this is my neighborhood too, and as long as I'm around, I want to help decide what happens to it.

Mo finally caught the high school pranksters who were messing with his diner and has Marcus fixing up the side of the building that was ruined.

As an apology for wrongfully accusing Danny, Mo is giving him a whole month of unlimited curly fries! Luckily, friend privileges means I get to enjoy free fries too.

It's even been busy for us here at Smiley's Cleaners!

Uncle Ott grumbles about how he can't keep track of it all, but new customers are good for business, so I know he doesn't actually mind. My parents still work all the time, but I've been helping out more too.

I used to think having a sketchbook would make me an artist, but I didn't completely feel like one until now. Maybe sharing your art with others makes it seem more real.

When Marcus walks into Smiley's this week, instead of just picking up laundry for Mo's Diner like he usually does, he points to my poster in the window.

It means a lot that he notices it— that he sees me as an artist too.

Then I find out that Marcus is planning to paint a mural on the blank wall he fixed up for Mo's Diner.

Truth is, I didn't always think of myself as an artist.

When Ms. Jenkins gave me my first sketchbook, I wasn't sure what to do with it.

Me? Art? I don't know...

What do you think?

Nisha was the one who made it seem like a good idea.

YOU'D BE A GREAT ARTIST!

Really?

She had a way of seeing people and really understanding them.

You always notice things. Now just try and draw them!

Maybe you're right...

Especially ME.

But where do I even start?!?!

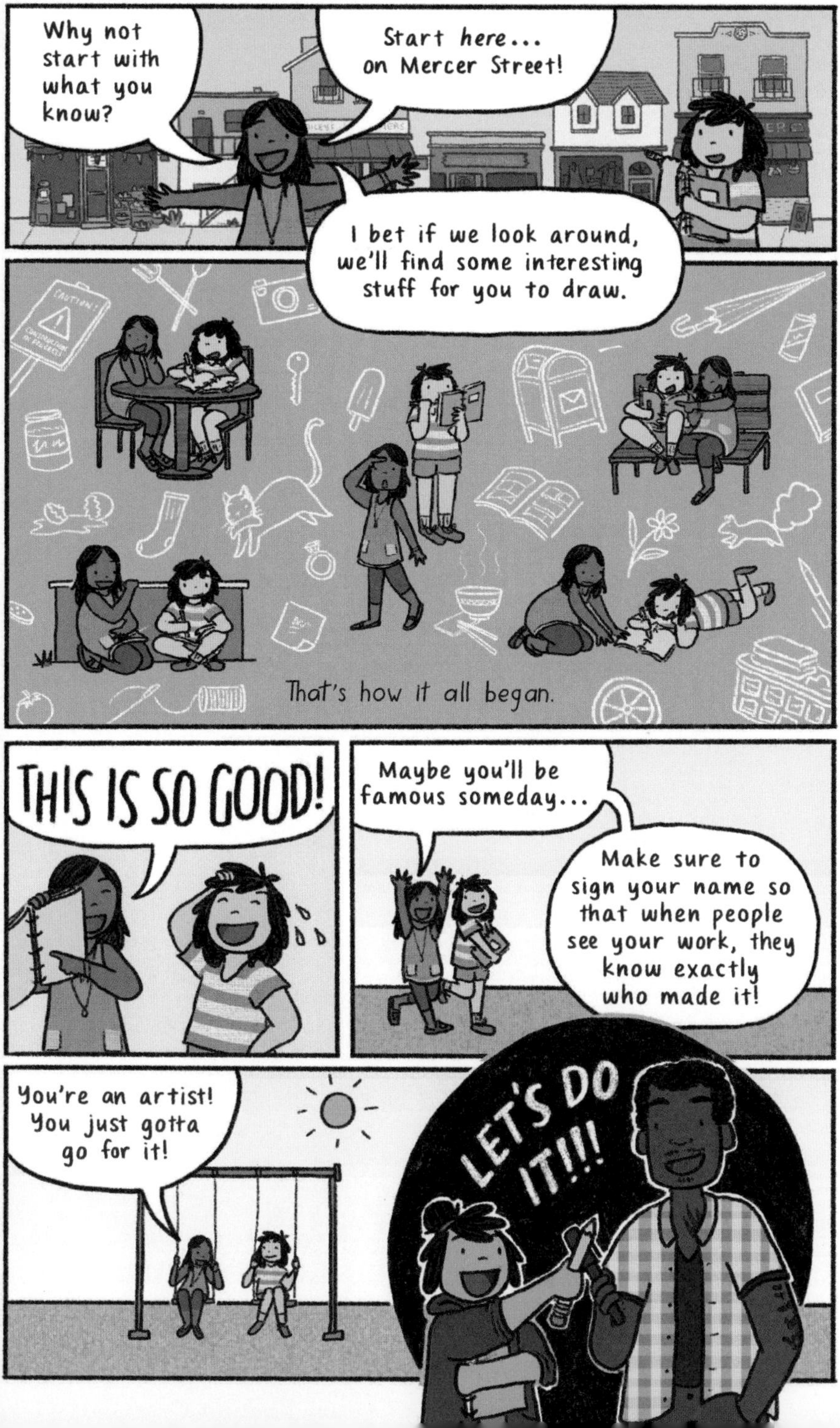
Why not start with what you know?
Start here... on Mercer Street!
I bet if we look around, we'll find some interesting stuff for you to draw.
That's how it all began.
THIS IS SO GOOD!
Maybe you'll be famous someday...
Make sure to sign your name so that when people see your work, they know exactly who made it!
You're an artist! You just gotta go for it!
LET'S DO IT!!!

I used to think being an artist meant capturing the world exactly as it is.
But I'm learning that it can also be about imagining the world as you want it to be.
I want it to be about Mercer Street...something that shows that this neighborhood isn't just buildings on a street.
It's a community. OUR community.

I don't know exactly what that will look like,
but I want to be part of making it happen.

CHAPTER 19

The Mercer Street block party is becoming a bigger deal than I expected. Once more people in the neighborhood started getting involved, it's just kept growing and growing.

Danny and I convinced some kids from school to help out too!

I brought snacks!

I never thought I'd have anything in common with them, but now I do.

Even the Bench Grandpas are doing their part!

Sign our petition!

The neighborhood around me is changing, but how I look at our neighborhood is changing too.

I used to think I knew everything about everyone. When you spend as much time observing others as I do, it's easy to forget how much you *can't* see.

But now this block party is bringing out sides of my neighbors that I never saw before!

Pam, the school bus driver, plays drums in a punk-rock cover band

Mr. Xin is the county's undefeated pepper-eating champion

Ms. Dascha makes and sells miniature felt animals

Mr. Becker has a bajillion grandchildren

Ms. Davis does stand-up comedy at least once a week

Mo used to be a professional ballroom dancer

Uncle Ott is a high-ranked competitive gamer

Maybe it's bringing out a different side of ME too.

I've heard people say that this is more than just a block party. I didn't know what they meant before, but I think I get it now.

It's not just a way to help the community garden or show off the new mural.

It's also a chance for everyone in the neighborhood to come together.

Well, *almost* everyone.

Sometimes it all just reminds me of
Nisha and the fact that she's not here.

We have so many memories
together on Mercer Street.
I know she would've loved
the idea of a neighborhood
block party. In fact, she
would've been the first
person to sign up to help.

Nisha may not live here anymore, but to me,
she'll always be part of the neighborhood.

She'll always be
my best friend.

I keep trying to reach her but still haven't had any luck. It's hard not to get frustrated.

So much for technology keeping people connected!

There *has* to be another way.

I think about all the things I want to say and all the things I want to ask. I don't know if I'll be able to fit it all in a letter . . .

Dear Nisha . . .

But when I finally try, all that *really* matters is seeing how she's doing and telling her how much I miss her.

I know she'll want an update on everything that has happened since she left. So I start with Mercer Street . . .

. . . and the rest just unfolds.

On the way to drop my letter off at the post office,
I pass by the mural to check on its progress.

Even though it's not
finished yet, there's enough
there to see the possibility
of something new.

Marcus says that when we're done, it should feel like it's part of the neighborhood, like it belongs to Mercer Street and everyone who lives here.

I like that.

Maybe *this* is the sort of change the Bench Grandpas always talk about needing—change that feels right, change that means something, change that we create for ourselves.

In my letter, I told Nisha all about it, but I hope one day, she'll get to come back and see for herself.

I think she'd like it too.

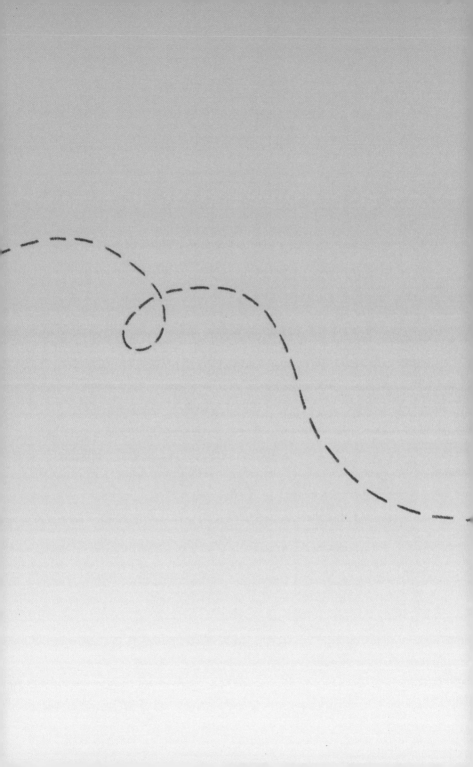

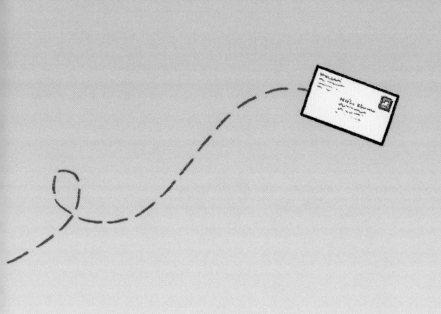

CHAPTER 20

The day before the block party, Marcus and I are working on the finishing touches for the mural.

It's a wonderful way to celebrate the community!

We love it.

The Mercer Street mural is right in the center of everything. Anyone who spends time in the neighborhood will see it . . .

Heading to the post office or the hair dresser . . .

Waiting in line for paletas . . .

Going to the park to play baseball . . .

Even riding the B52 bus that runs through town.

In a way, the mural isn't just about Mercer Street—it's PART of it, too.

Once we clean up all the rough edges and wait for the paint to dry, the last thing is for Marcus to sign it.

So he picks up a brush, and scribbles his name in the corner. Then he hands it to ME.

C'mon! We did this together.

This feels big—bigger than the mural itself (which is pretty big already).

In a way, putting my name on that wall makes me feel like *I'm* part of Mercer Street too.

When I look up, I know that I helped make something new for our neighborhood.

I think that's the best thing about being an artist. You get to add something to the world that wasn't there before.

When the day arrives, our block party ends up being a huge success!

People are coming from all over to see what's happening on Mercer Street.

Wherever you look, there's some sort of cool craft for sale or delicious new food to try or fun performance going on.

It really is like a celebration!

This all may seem exciting and new, but if I really think about it, the things that make the block party great have always been here on Mercer Street. I just didn't appreciate them before.

I never used to think there was anything particularly interesting about our neighborhood.

But now when I look a little closer, I can see that there has always been something special here . . .

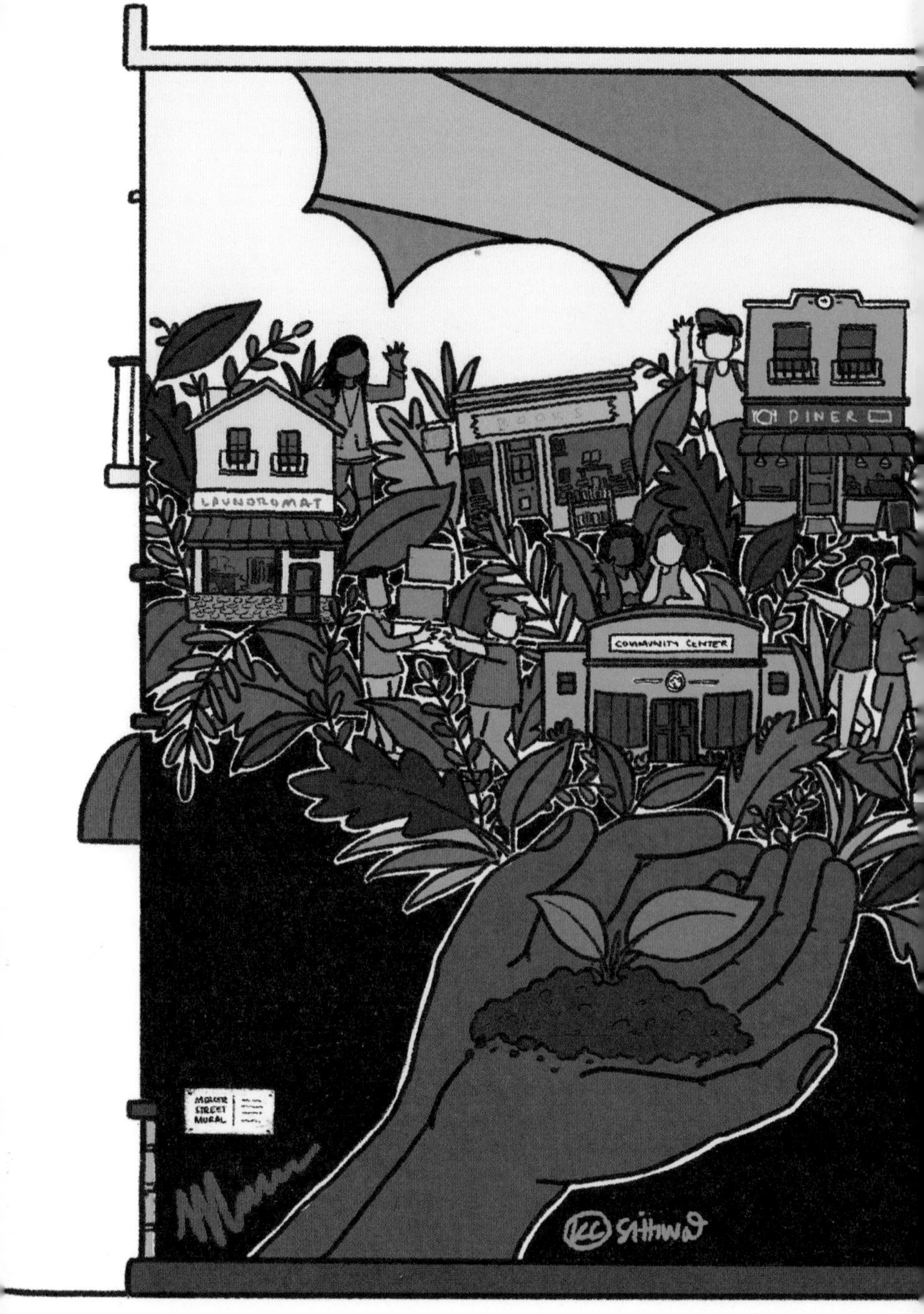
LAUNDROMAT
DINER
COMMUNITY CENTER
STREET MURAL

And that's something worth holding on to.

ACKNOWLEDGMENTS

Editor	Jenne Abramowitz
Agent	Steven Malk
Colorist	Joan Wirolinggo
Design	Cassy Price
	Christopher Stengel
Production	Janell Harris
Marketing	Rachel Feld
	Katie Dutton
	Lizette Serrano
Publicity	Aleah Gornbein
Sales	The whole Scholastic team

A book is the collective effort of so many people. Thank you to everyone at Scholastic for helping me bring Mercer Street to life!

The Mercer Street in this book is not based off any one specific place, but rather, a collection of neighborhoods I've known and a feeling of community I always hope to find no matter where I am.

Without my own community of friends and family, this book could not exist. A special shout-out to the early readers and supporters of Mercer Street: Tae, Lauren, Alia, and Chucalo Finally, thanks to all the booksellers, educators, and readers who have made space for me on your shelves over the years. I couldn' ask for a better community.